Sábana the Sloth

Cristina Sicard
Illustrated by Sarah de Camps

Copyright © 2020 Cristina Sicard
Copyright © 2020 Monday Creek Publishing
All Rights Reserved

ISBN 978-0-578-71661-9

Monday Creek Publishing LLC
mondaycreekpublishing.com

To our wonderful Guillo,

We want you to know this is part of your legacy.

Guillo, you were special, and you were here for a purpose. You have the biggest heart.

Love you always,
Your Mami and your big sister Cristina

Acknowledgments

Professor Carolyn Embree,
Lucky and grateful for your knowledge and empathy towards this story.
Thank you for the care you give to everyone.

To the Reader,
Life has its problems, yet remember the "courage to continue is so worthwhile."
Thank you for supporting *Sábana the Sloth*. No matter the times, make sure to support yourself and others.

What a delightful day for sloths to sleep.
But if you listen closely,
you can hear one weep.

Sábana's tears splash over his face while he hangs upside down.

"Why do I worry about everything?" he says, hoping no one is around.

Year after year, Sábana's mind makes him feel a mess.
Climbing down the tree once a week to potty is too much stress.

Lula climbs over the piles of clothes and onto her rocking chair.
Even when she stumbles and falls, her mind stays clear.

As Lula dashes down the dirt, parrots squawk and monkeys chime.

Once Lula gets to the water she shouts, "What will I climb?"

Lula leaps into the whooshing waves.
The water is icy cold – *ahh*, she is so brave!

Using his crayon-length claws to squeeze Pinky, he moves up.
HONK! A truck swerves near his tree splashing water – ahhh, heads-up!

Lula, on her way home, sprints over to check in.

"¡Hola!" she calls out to her new friend.

"Here's your sábana rosada," she extends.

"Gracias, me llamo Sábana," he grins.

"Y yo, Lula," she begins.

"Why do you live in a tree so close to the ground?"
Where to begin with my million fears all around?

Talking about what scares Sábana out loud is never easy, really.
But he wants his mind to be strong, so he can live freely.

"I live low to the ground because I am scared of heights.
I am also super scared of noise and water, alright?"

"Sábana, it is okay. I am going to help; you stay."

Lula returns to bring Sábana some company.

"The first helper is a drum to make you feel more harmony."

"Anybody who hears one of these can listen to any ring."

Ba-bam, ba-bam, ba-bam!

How can this noisy noise be a real thing?

It sounds like a bunch of monkeys.

"*EEEEEEEEE,*" Sábana almost flees.

"That's okay. Let's try and work on your climbing," Lula suggests.
She comes back with her rocking chair for the test.

"If you practice climbing this,
you won't be so scared of heights."

"EEEEEEEEE," Sábana can't make it past his fright.

"No hay problema, let me bring una piscina," Lula smiles.
Dragging her inflatable pool, she tells Sábana, "Water scared me as a child.

When I was niña, I ran from waves like you."

It doesn't matter. "EEEEEEEEE," Sábana feels blue.

Hours go by and Sábana hasn't moved.

Lula waits while Sábana tries to improve.

Nighttime is here and Lula starts to cry.
"I didn't realize the time and now it's a dark sky."

"Lula, you're scared of the dark?"
"I am..." Then, her face sparks.

"Sábana, you're not afraid of the dark!" Lula waves.

"You do have more fears than most, yet you're still brave."

"Muchas gracias," Sábana calls out as Lula hurries back to her home.

I am brave for trying so many things today outside my comfort zone.

Always Learning
Siempre Aprendiendo

The Sicard de Camps Reading
Los Sicard de Camps Leyendo

GLOSSARY
GLOSARIO

¡Hola!	Hello!
sábana	sheet
rosada	pink
Gracias	Thank you
me llamo	my name is
Y yo	And I
No hay problema	No problem
una piscina	a pool
niña	little girl
Muchas gracias	Thank you very much

Sarah de Camps and Cristina Sicard

About the Author
Cristina Sicard, children's author who brought you the lovable llama *Harmony*, carries on wanting to help children and adults alike through compelling storytelling. Resembling Cristina's own battles with mental health, Sábana and Lula are characters she hopes connect with individuals and elevate diversity and inclusion. To calm her worries, Cristina loves to take walks in the sunshine, laugh at herself and the messages her Dominican family sends in WhatsApp, pose with her gorgeous cat Cloudy, dance in front of mirrors, and work on projects with her out of this world Mami.

About the Illustrator
Sarah de Camps never dreamed of illustrating a children's book. The moment she chose to study medicine, she knew it had to be pediatrics. As a pediatrician, Dr. de Camps believes kids are tesoros or treasures. Sarah loves how special it is to recuperate children and bring joy to families. She picked up painting with watercolors as a way to heal after her son's passing. Sarah feels emotional completing a book with her daughter Cristina to support others and honor Guillo.

CPSIA information can be obtained
at www.ICGtesting.com
Printed in the USA
LVRC092335190821
695736LV00003B/73